SAMMY SPIDER'S
FIRST
YOM KIPPUR

This
PJ BOOK
belongs to

_____

_____

PJ Library®

JEWISH BEDTIME STORIES and SONGS

Sylvia A. Rouss

Illustrated by
Katherine Janus Kahn

KAR-BEN
PUBLISHING

To my loving family who always show kindness and caring for others: Jeff, Gabby, Todd, Hayden, Derek, Leo, Shannan, Jordan, and Allegra.

—S.A.R.

For my dear friends Bob and Hazel Keimowitz; their daughters Jessica and Alison, the lovely models for my first book *The Passover Parrot*; for the new generation, Hannah and Miriam Crozier and Noa and Abraham Spodek; and in loving memory of David Crozier.

—K.J.K.

Text copyright © 2013 by Sylvia A. Rouss
Illustrations copyright © 2013 by Katherine Janus Kahn

KAR-BEN PUBLISHING
A division of Lerner Publishing Group, Inc.
241 First Avenue North
Minneapolis, MN 55401 U.S.A.
1-800-4-Karben

Website address: www.karben.com

Library of Congress Cataloging-in-Publication Data

Rouss, Sylvia A.
    Sammy Spider's first Yom Kippur/ by Sylvia A. Rouss ;
 illustrated by Katherine Janus Kahn.
      p.   cm.
    Summary: "Sammy Spider learns about the Jewish holiday
 Yom Kippur."—Provided by publisher
    ISBN 978–0–7613–9195–1 (lib. bdg. : alk. paper)
    ISBN 978–1–4677–1639–0 (eBook)
    [1. Yom Kippur—Fiction. 2. Spiders—Fiction.]
 I. Kahn, Katherine, ill. II. Title.
 PZ7.R7622Say 2013
 [E]—dc23   2012029132

Manufactured in Hong Kong
3 – PN – 4/1/15

081511.5K2/B0723/A3

Sammy Spider was relaxing in his web on the Shapiros' living room ceiling. Suddenly, Josh burst through the front door blowing a horn he had made at school. Sammy jumped at the loud noise.

"Mother," shouted Sammy.
"What is Josh blowing?"

"That's a shofar, Sammy. The rabbi blows a shofar at Rosh Hashanah services to welcome the New Year. The shofar is also sounded at the end of Yom Kippur."

"What's Yom Kippur?" asked Sammy.

"Yom Kippur is a holy day when people tell each other they are sorry for saying or doing something hurtful. On Yom Kippur, Josh's family will spend the day in synagogue praying. Mr. and Mrs. Shapiro won't eat until services are over at the end of the day."

"Will we go to synagogue, too?" asked Sammy.

"Silly little Sammy. Spiders don't go to synagogue. Spiders spin webs," answered Mrs. Spider.

Josh placed his little shofar under the honey dish, next to the family's large, curvy shofar.

"Can I have a shofar to blow?" pleaded Sammy.

Mrs. Spider laughed. "Silly little Sammy. Spiders don't blow shofars. Spiders spin webs."

Sammy lowered himself on a strand of webbing to get a closer look at the shofar, when Mrs. Shapiro asked Josh, "How was school today?"

"I have homework," Josh said. "My teacher wants us to make a list of all the people we should apologize to before Yom Kippur. Will you help me write the list?"

"We'll do it after dinner," Mrs. Shapiro suggested. "While I set the table, why don't you put your toys away? Your ball belongs outside."

Josh picked up his ball. He bounced it on the floor, and Sammy scrambled up his web as the ball came towards him.

Josh dribbled the ball a
few times and bounced it
even harder. Sammy's web
began to shake. He felt like he
was on a trampoline.

Mr. and Mrs. Shapiro rushed in
to see what the noise was.

As Josh's ball took
a final bounce, it hit a
shelf, knocking the honey
dish to the floor. Sammy's
web snapped loose.

"What happened?" his parents asked.

Josh looked frightened. "I was playing ball
and it hit the shelf. It was an accident. I
didn't mean to do it!" he said. As he spoke,
he noticed two little spiders scurrying away.

Mr. Shapiro looked at Josh sternly.
"Don't you remember the rules?
The ball is an outside toy."

Josh nodded tearfully.

"Then please take
it outside and get a
broom," his dad said.

Sammy and Mrs. Spider climbed back up to the ceiling and began spinning themselves a new web. Josh swept the glass from the floor and gently replaced the shofars on the shelf.

Mrs. Shapiro looked at Josh. "Now please pick up your toys so we can have dinner. Then we can work on the list of people you want to apologize to before Yom Kippur."

As Josh hurried to put his toys away, he looked up at the ceiling. The two spiders were busy spinning a web.

After dinner, Josh sat on the couch with
his parents. Mrs. Shapiro was holding a
note pad and a pen.

"Who is first on your list?" she asked.
Josh looked at his parents.

"Both of you," he whispered sadly.

"I'm sorry I didn't put away my
toys when you asked me.

"I'm sorry I played ball in the house when I knew I shouldn't.

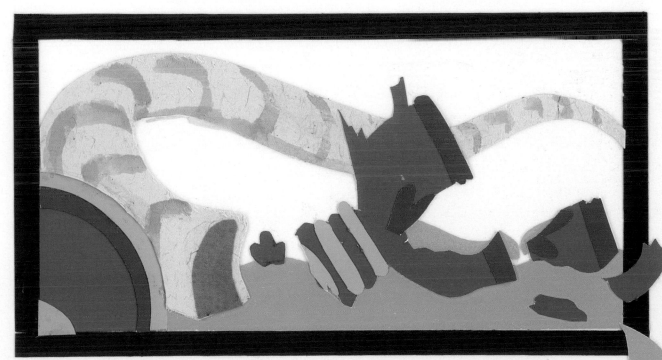

"And I'm sorry I broke the honey dish and knocked the shofars off the shelf."

Josh's parents gave him a hug.
"We accept your apology," they said.

"There's one more thing I want
to add to the list," said Josh,
looking up.

"I'm sorry I broke
your web, little spiders."

Sammy looked at his mother and smiled. "I think we should accept his apology," he said.

About Yom Kippur

Yom Kippur, the Day of Atonement, is the holiest day of the Jewish year. It is a day of forgiveness and repentance, when Jews the world over fast and pray. Before Yom Kippur it is traditional to ask forgiveness and to seek reconciliation from those one has wronged.

About the Author

Sylvia A. Rouss is the award-winning author of over 20 children's books, including the popular *Sammy Spider* series. She wrote *The Littlest Pair*, which won the National Jewish Book Award and *Sammy Spider's First Trip to Israel*, which was named a Sydney Taylor Honor book by the Association of Jewish Libraries. She teaches preschool at the Stephen S. Wise Temple in Los Angeles.

About the Illustrator

Katherine Janus Kahn has illustrated more than 30 picture books, toddler board books, holiday services, and activity books for Kar-Ben. She and Sammy Spider frequently visit schools and bookstores for storytelling and chalk talks. She also paints and sculpts. She lives in Wheaton, MD.